This book must be returned by the date specified at the time of issue as the DUE DATE FOR RETURN
The loan may be extended (personally, by post, telephone or online) for a further period, if the book is not required by another reader, by quoting the barcode / author / title.

Enquiries: 01709 336774

www.rotherham.gov.uk/libraries

With special thanks to Tabitha Jones

For Joshua Bartlett

ORCHARD BOOKS

First published in Great Britain in 2017 by The Watts Publishing Group

1 3 5 7 9 10 8 6 4 2

Text © 2017 Beast Quest Limited.
Cover and inside illustrations by Steve Sims
© Beast Quest Limited 2017

Beast Quest is a registered trademark of Beast Quest Limited
Series created by Beast Quest Limited, London

A CIP catalogue record for this book is available from the British Library.

ISBN 978 1 40834 311 1

Printed and bound by CPI Group (UK) Ltd, Croydon, CR0 4YY

Orchard Books
An imprint of Hachette Children's Group
Part of The Watts Publishing Group Limited
Carmelite House, 50 Victoria Embankment, London EC4Y 0DZ

An Hachette UK Company
www.hachette.co.uk
www.hachettechildrens.co.uk

QuarG
THE STONE DRAGON

BY ADAM BLADE

ORCHARD

CONTENTS

When I was a young apprentice wizard, there was a secret chamber my master forbade me to enter. But even then, I did not like being told what to do. With a simple unlocking spell, I found my way in.

I was very disappointed. For that room contained no potions or poisons, no magical weapons. All I saw was a single oval stone, grey and speckled, lying on a cushion.

My master found me. To my surprise, he did not beat or curse me. Instead he smiled.

"Jezrin," he said, "behold the key to immeasurable power!"

"What, an old rock?" I replied.

At that, his face turned grave. "That is no rock, apprentice. That is a dragon egg. And one day it will allow you to spread Evil to every corner of every kingdom."

As he led me from the room, I was not impressed. My master never lived to see the egg hatch. But his promise proved true.

The time of Evil has come. And nothing – no one – can stand in my path.

A TERRIBLE
HOMECOMING

Tom's body swayed gently in time
with Storm's hoofbeats. In the
saddle behind him, Elenna let out a
contented yawn. Feathery streaks of
pink and gold painted the evening
sky. The fierce heat of the day had
ebbed as they rode. A welcome
breeze, sweet with the smell of sun-

baked grass, cooled the sweat on Tom's face.

Avantia had been so calm since Tom and Elenna completed their latest Quest that King Hugo had granted them leave to visit Tom's home village, Errinel. Excitement swelled in Tom's chest at the thought of seeing his aunt and uncle again. He spotted a swift shadow loping towards them across the fields. A moment later Silver, Elenna's wolf, took his place at Storm's side.

"Hello, boy!" Elenna said. "Did you catch anything good?"

Silver looked up at her, his eyes bright points in the gloom. He licked his muzzle.

"I'll take that as a yes," Elenna said. "I could do with some supper too! It's getting late. Do you think we should set up camp?"

Tom shook his head. "If we press on, we should reach Errinel before Aunt Maria and Uncle Henry turn in – maybe even in time for dinner."

"Sounds good to me," Elenna said. "I'd much prefer to sleep in a bed tonight than on the ground."

They followed the road onwards, past darkening fields and dusky copses of trees echoing with the melodies of hidden birds. Gradually, everything fell silent about them except for the steady clop of Storm's hooves. Stars blinked into life one by one until the wide, moonless sky glittered with their light.

Tom flexed his tired shoulders as Storm rounded the last bend of their journey. The lights of his village came into view, along with the comforting sight of chimney smoke curling into the sky. But as they neared Errinel, Tom felt his horse's steps falter and slow. Storm's head went up and his ears flicked back. Tom squeezed Storm's flanks with his knees.

"Keep going, boy," he said. "There are oats and a cosy stable ahead!"

Behind them, Silver let out an uneasy growl. Tom glanced back to see the wolf's hackles raised and his sharp teeth bared.

"What's up, Silver?" Elenna asked.

Tom couldn't see anything ahead except the silhouettes of houses, broken by the soft glow of doors and windows left open to let in the warm night air.

"We'd best be on our guard," Elenna said.

Tom nodded and loosened his sword in its sheath. As Storm passed between the first cottages, the sound of the stallion's hoof beats echoed strangely. Tom's skin prickled.

"It's too quiet," he said.

He pulled Storm to a halt and dropped from the saddle with Elenna at his side. They signalled for the animals to wait and crossed to the nearest cottage. As they entered, Tom heard the rustle of last embers of a dying fire settling in the grate. The guttering light from a candle stub cast bobbing shadows across the walls.

"Hello?" Tom called. But his voice fell dead in the empty silence. He and Elenna exchanged puzzled frowns.

"Let's try the next house," Elenna said.

There, plates of food lay half eaten on the table. The dining chairs had been pushed back crookedly, and a pitcher of water lay on its side, spilling a dark puddle on to the floor.

"Where is everyone?" Elenna asked.
Tom's pulse quickened. "Let's try
the forge," he said. As they stepped
back into the night, the tang of

sweet, acrid smoke caught in Tom's throat. He frowned. *Burning sugar?*

The smell grew stronger as he and Elenna followed the deserted street. Soon Tom could see smoke billowing from the open door of his uncle's cottage. His heart gave a skip of fear.

I hope Henry and Maria are all right.

He and Elenna rushed inside to find smoke streaming from around the edge of the stove door. Tom threw it open. More smoke billowed out, stinging his eyes. When it cleared, Tom saw a blackened pie.

What's going on here?

"Everyone can't have just vanished!" he said.

Elenna glanced about the cottage, frowning. "Nothing's been damaged," she said. "And I don't see any sign of a Beast attack or any dark magic. The fact that no one's here might be a good sign. Whatever happened, everyone escaped."

Tom took in the familiar details of his aunt's tidy kitchen and the table set with butter and jam. *Elenna's right*, he told himself. But still, he couldn't shake the worry gnawing inside him.

"Let's check the town hall," he said. "Maybe everyone's there."

He and Elenna left the forge behind, passing more empty houses and deserted side streets, until they

reached the main square. Apart from
the quiet bubbling of the town's
stone fountain, silence greeted them.
The windows of the town hall shone
darkly in the flickering torchlight
that lit the square...

And in its shadow, a dark silhouette
was crouched.

"Hello?" Tom called.

The figure didn't stir. Tom pulled
a torch from its holder and started
towards the hooded figure, his hand on

the hilt of his sword. Whoever it was remained frozen, their arms thrust out before them, as if warding off an attack. When Tom reached the figure, the light from his torch fell on robes of hard, grey stone.

"It's a statue!" Elenna said.

Tom frowned. "But why put it here? It's practically blocking the door to the hall."

Elenna circled the statue, peering at its features. She gasped. "Tom! Look!"

Tom stepped to Elenna's side. As his torch fell on the statue's face, his stomach lurched. The statue was staring ahead, wide-eyed with terror, its mouth open, as if in mid-

shout. But Tom recognised its broad
cheekbones and mischievous, cat-
like eyes.

Petra!

2

STONE WITCH

Tom stared at the strange statue of the young witch. Despite their difficult past, Tom had begun to regard Petra as a friend – at least when she wasn't teasing him. Nothing about the stone carving made any sense. He reached out a hand to touch it. A muffled cry seemed to come from inside. Tom snatched back his hand.

"Petra's in there!" he said.

The cry came again. Tom couldn't make out any words, but he could hear the panic in Petra's voice.

"Can you break the stone with your sword?" Elenna said.

"Not without risking hurting her," Tom said. "Wait here. I'll get a chisel." Tom raced to the forge. He returned to see Elenna beckoning frantically.

"Hurry!" Elenna said. "I think she's in real trouble!" Petra's cries had turned to high, panicked yelps.

Tom set his chisel against the statue's hood and tapped it with his hammer. A chip of rock flaked away. He tried again, knocking off another splinter of rock, then another. Petra's cries were getting more desperate by the moment. Tom raised his hammer.

Smack! He brought it down with all his strength.

Cracks appeared across the statue, spreading quickly from where he'd struck. A chunk of stone fell away, revealing the soft fabric of Petra's hood. Tom tore away more stone with his hands, peeling the rock from Petra's face while Elenna prised chunks from her shoulders and arms.

As soon as Petra's nose and mouth were free, she drew in a loud gasp of breath, then coughed and spluttered. Tom and Elenna kept tugging away more stone. Petra helped, raking at

the stone with her fingers. Before
long, she stepped from the remains
of the statue, spitting out a mouthful
of dust. Finally she turned to Tom,
her cheeks flushed and her eyes
bright in her dust-streaked face.

"Thank you!" she said. "I was

almost out of air!"

Tom felt a rush of relief at seeing Petra safe, but it quickly gave way to anger and worry. Wherever Petra went, trouble usually followed. He grabbed her by the shoulders.

"What have you done?" he asked.

Petra frowned and pushed him away. "What have *I* done?" she asked. "Only put my life on the line to save your village. I warned everyone to leave. If it wasn't for me, they'd all be statues." Petra pouted and looked at her feet. "I guess that's the thanks I deserve for being stupid enough to think I could battle Quarg by myself."

Tom and Elenna exchanged a

worried look. "Quarg?" Tom said.

Petra rolled her eyes at Tom as if he were slow, then pointed up past him into the starry sky. "Yes – Quarg," she said. "That dirty great dragon headed our way. He's a mean shot too, so you might want to move."

Tom turned to see a vast black shape with broad wings and a long spiked tail swooping towards him, blocking out the stars. The dragon had cruel-looking curved talons tucked up under his belly and sharp horns jutting from above blazing eyes.

"A Beast!" Elenna cried, reaching for her bow and arrows.

Tom lifted his sword and leapt

in front of Elenna and Petra. The dragon dived towards him. Torchlight flickered across his inky scales, and Tom saw they were not black, but deep, dark purple. He let out a roar, blasting Tom with the stench of rotting meat, making the ground shudder. *Thwack!* One of Elenna's arrows whizzed past Tom and bounced off the dragon's scales without leaving a mark. Tom squared his shoulders as the Beast's smouldering gaze met his.

"Watch out!" Petra cried, yanking Tom sharply back by the arm as two purple jets of crackling flame shot from Quarg's eyes.

Crack! The energy beams struck the ground right where Tom had been

standing, showering him with earth.

"Take cover!" Petra cried. Elenna
dived behind the square's stone
fountain, but Tom stood his ground,

preparing to catch the next blast with Ferno's scale. Quarg wheeled around and swooped down. His yellow eyes gleamed and his lipless mouth curled in a toothy smile. Tom tensed his muscles, ready...

"Oh, for goodness' sake!" Petra grabbed Tom's tunic and jerked him back behind the fountain with Elenna.

BOOM! The sound of stone hitting stone filled the air.

"Hey!" Tom cried, rounding on Petra. "What are you doing?"

Petra frowned, her hands on her hips. "You saved my life," she said. "I'm returning the favour. Your silly dragon scale won't help you this time. Quarg's jets aren't flame – they're what turned me to stone! And there's something else you'd better see." Petra leaned over, peering out from behind the stone fountain, then beckoned Tom to her side.

Elenna craned her neck to look round them. Quarg hovered above the square. The dragon's massive wings beat the air, buffeting them with a fierce wind, making Tom squint. His eyes blazed the fierce electric blue of lightning. High on the Beast's back, Tom spotted the slender figure of a boy with a long, billowing cloak.

"Who's that?" Elenna said.

Tom called on the power of his

golden helmet, and focused in on the figure, his vision growing keen and sharp from the helmet's magic. A glimpse of white hair and ice-blue eyes beneath the shadow of a grey hood confirmed his fears. It was Jezrin's evil apprentice.

"Berric!" Tom said.

PETRA'S TALE

Tom, Elenna and Petra crouched behind the stone fountain, the sound of Quarg's mighty wingbeats loud above them.

"I should have known Berric wouldn't lie low for long!" Tom growled.

"At least we got here in time to defend the village," Elenna said.

"Ahem!" Petra said. "*Who* got here in time?"

Elenna rolled her eyes. "You'd still be a statue if it wasn't for us," she said.

Crack! Purple light flared around them and chunks of stone rained down from above.

"Ow!" Petra cried, shrinking closer to the fountain, holding a hand to her head.

Tom glanced up to see a section of the curved stone missing from the fountain's wide bowl, and water trickling to the ground.

"Get under here before Quarg fires again," he said, throwing his shield above them. The three of them huddled in the darkness, so close together Tom could hear the anxious rasp of the girls' breathing.

"What now?" Petra hissed.

"Now it's time to send that big lizard packing," Elenna said.

"Don't look at me!" Petra said. "I'm done being a hero today."

Elenna slid her bow from her back. "I have an idea," she said. She stepped back, grabbed the stone rim of the fountain's cracked basin, then vaulted up on to it.

Tom stepped out behind her to watch. "Be careful!" he said. "That dragon could turn you to stone in an instant!"

Quarg's eyes flashed as his gaze

fell on Elenna. The great dragon tipped his wings and swooped towards her, flying so low Tom could make out the wide grin on Berric's pale face as he clung to Quarg's back. Elenna notched an arrow and took aim. Tom's chest tightened with fear as the Beast drew closer, his fiery gaze on his friend.

Elenna let her arrow fly, then leapt down beside Tom just as twin blasts of purple flame shot from the dragon's eyes, blowing the stone where she'd been standing to dust. Berric yelped and lurched sideways, grabbing his shoulder and almost toppling from the dragon's back. Elenna's arrow clattered to

the ground in the distance, and
Tom knew it must only have grazed
Berric's flesh. But still, Berric lifted
his arm and pointed towards the
eastern horizon.

"Away!" he cried.

Quarg flapped his mighty wings, quickly gaining height, and soon vanished into the night sky.

"Good shot!" Tom said.

Elenna dusted her hands together, grinning. "I didn't think Berric would stick about for long after that!"

Petra shrugged. "He probably just figured his job here is already done," she said.

"What do you mean?" Tom asked.

"Are you really that dim?" Petra said, her eyes shining. "Jezrin sent Berric as a decoy. He knew you'd be coming to Errinel, and wanted Berric to keep you distracted."

"But why?" Tom asked.

Petra spread her hands wide. "So no one could stop him drinking from the Well of Power, of course," she said.

Tom frowned and shook his head. "I've never even heard of the Well of Power."

"Not many people have," Petra said, inspecting her bitten nails. "In fact, even I thought it was a myth until recently. It's not in Avantia. It lies east, beyond the Forbidden Lands, in a realm called Drakonia – the Kingdom of Dragons. The only way to reach it is by flying on a dragon. Jezrin's gone there to find the well. And I'll bet Berric's headed that way, too."

"For something you thought was only a myth, you seem to know rather a lot about it," Elenna said. "And about Jezrin's plans. How do we know you're not working for him?"

Petra let out a long sigh. "You found me suffocating inside a stone block, remember?" she said. "Does it sound like I'm on Jezrin's side?"

"No," Tom said. "But in that case, how do you know what he's up to?"

Petra grinned and tipped her face to the sky. She lifted her hands to her lips and let out a grating squawk that made Tom grimace.

An answering caw came from a shadowy cluster of trees on a hill

beyond the village. Tom heard the
flap of wings. A moment later, a huge
crow landed on Petra's shoulder. The
bird's wings gleamed dark ruby red
in the torchlight. It cocked its head
then nibbled the tip of Petra's ear,

before letting out another raucous, rasping caw. "Clever Petra!"

"This is my new best friend, Rourke," Petra said, stroking the satiny feathers of the bird's neck. "I've cast a spell on him that allows me to see through his eyes. We've been spying on Jezrin!"

Tom raised an eyebrow. "Impressive," he said.

Elenna shrugged. "Creepy, if you ask me. And we've still got to stop Jezrin and Berric. How are we even going to get to Drakonia?"

It was Tom's turn to grin. "Well, don't we have our own dragon here in Avantia?" He touched his fingers to the red jewel in his belt, feeling it instantly grow warm. *Ferno, come to us!*

"Tom!" a familiar voice called. Tom turned to see his Uncle Henry peering from the town hall door. He emerged with Maria at his side, followed by several other villagers.

Tom hurried forwards to meet his aunt and uncle, relieved to see everyone safe. Henry folded him and Elenna in a bear hug. Once he'd released them, he ran his eyes over the crater blasted in the square, and the damaged fountain.

He turned to Petra. "It looks like we owe you our thanks," he said.

Petra grinned. "I'd prefer supper, if it's all the same!" she said.

At Henry's side, Maria shrugged apologetically. "I'm afraid supper's ruined." Maria turned to Tom. "I am so sorry. I know you've been looking forward to some home-cooked food."

Tom smiled. "We can't stay now, anyway," he said. "There's an Evil Wizard and a Beast on the loose. But if you could look after Storm and Silver until we get back, and find us some supplies for the journey, that would be very welcome."

Henry put his big hand on Tom's shoulder and looked him sternly in the eye. "I saw that dragon," Henry said. "You be careful on this Quest."

Tom nodded gravely. A sudden breeze stirred the air, bringing with it the swish of vast wings. Tom looked up to see Ferno's magnificent form silhouetted against the night sky.

Cries of fear went up from the villagers crossing the square. Many started to run.

"Don't worry," Tom called. "Ferno is a Good Beast."

Despite Tom's words, the remaining villagers hurried away as the dragon came in to land. Ferno extended his talons and touched down, throwing up a cloud of dust. He folded his wings and turned his fiery gaze on Tom.

Tom put his hand to the red jewel in his belt. *Brave friend, I need*

passage to Drakonia, he told the dragon.

Ferno's orange eyes narrowed. He let out a snort of flame. *Drakonia is no place for humans*, he said gruffly, speaking into Tom's mind.

Nevertheless, I must go, Tom said. *I must protect Avantia from Jezrin's Evil.*

Ferno bowed his gigantic head.

As you wish, he said. *But I warn you, even I cannot protect you in the Kingdom of Dragons...*

THE KINGDOM OF DRAGONS

Tom, Elenna and Petra crouched side by side on Ferno's back, clinging to the dragon's scales. A cold wind buffeted against them as the dark landscape rolled by far below. The Good Beast carried them swiftly, but still Tom's body grew chill and numb long before the borders of Avantia drew near.

In the moonless dusk before dawn, the desolate plains of the Forbidden Lands spread out before them. Tom gazed down at the decaying landscape, half hidden by shrouds of mist. Craggy mountains jutted from the mist like rotten teeth, and the black skeleton hands of trees reached up into the night. A shiver of fear traced Tom's spine at the memory of his time spent in that forsaken place. Petra and Elenna huddled closer beside him.

Ferno soared over the deep shadow of the dead forest and beyond, further than Tom had ever travelled. Finally, a dim grey light crept into the eastern sky, revealing what looked like an endless plain of lifeless dust below.

An eerie silence settled around them, broken only by the mournful sweep of the wind across Ferno's wings.

Tom drew his cloak tight about him and cleared his throat. "Petra, do you know how Jezrin plans to find this Well of Power?" he asked.

The young witch shook herself awake from a half-doze. On her shoulder, Rourke flapped and scolded, then settled again as Petra frowned thoughtfully.

"There have always been rumours in magic circles that Jezrin's master once stole a dragon's egg and used

Evil magic to force it to hatch. Of course, everyone thought the story was a bluff put about by Jezrin. But after our adventures in Errinel, it seems that those rumours were true." Petra shrugged. "And what better way to get about Drakonia than adopting your own pet dragon?"

"I'd prefer a pet that wasn't likely to turn me to stone," Elenna said.

"Look!" Tom pointed up ahead. A wavering line of orange fire glimmered in the dawn sky, growing brighter by the moment. The fiery streak quickly widened to a swathe, writhing like a wound of flame in the half-darkness.

"That must be the gateway to

Drakonia!" Petra said.

Ferno beat his gigantic wings, banking steeply upwards towards the portal of flames. As they drew close, Tom felt a wave of heat hit him, bringing with it a stench like rotten eggs, smoke and ash. Tom bent his head into the scorching wind and clung tight to Ferno's scales.

Whumph! Bright tongues of fire crackled about them, then the desolate plain below vanished, replaced by a roiling mass of black lava laced with glowing orange streaks. Jagged rocks jutted up from the fiery sea of molten rock. Craggy mountains, belching plumes of black

smoke rose up all around them, and
forked lightning crackled across a
blanket of dark cloud above. Tom
could hardly catch his breath in
the smothering heat. A fierce sweat
broke out across his skin. Elenna
coughed and choked as they hit a

bank of tattered cloud. Acrid gases burned Tom's eyes and throat, and the gritty taste of ash filled his mouth.

"Look out ahead!" Petra said, jabbing Tom with her elbow and pointing.

Tom followed the line of her finger

with his eyes to see a black crust of lava swelling to a huge red bulge like a boil. Fear jolted though him. He tugged at Ferno's neck. The dragon tipped his wings, changing course in an instant. The bubble of lava exploded as they swerved past, sending a jet of white hot flame upwards, so close Tom felt the scalding heat of it on his skin.

Do you see now why you must turn back? Ferno said, speaking into Tom's mind.

Tom touched his fingers to his red jewel. *I see the danger, but the safety of Avantia and all the kingdoms is at stake. While there's blood in my veins, I can't turn back.*

Ferno let out a short growl – a note of grudging agreement. *In that case, hang on tight...*

The dragon beat his massive wings. The sudden acceleration snatched Tom's breath away. Petra and Elenna gasped and threw themselves down on to Ferno's scales. The fiery landscape melted into a blur of speed all around them. Spurts of flame and towers of jagged rock whooshed by on either side. Ferno tipped his wings, soaring and dipping low, then rising up on hot currents of putrid air. Tom squinted into the buffeting gusts, his stomach flipping with each drop and turn Ferno made. Lightning flickered above them and thunder echoed all around alongside the rumbling *boom* of erupting volcanoes.

Suddenly two arching plumes of fire shot towards them from either side. Ferno tipped, flinging one wing up and the other down, veering sharply between the deadly spurts. Elenna slammed into Tom, sliding on Ferno's scales, but then managed to catch her balance. On Tom's other side, Petra yelped and grabbed his arm to keep from slipping into the fiery sea. Rourke flapped and screeched.

Tom gritted his teeth and braced himself against Petra's weight. The

young witch dug her fingers into his
flesh, holding on with a desperate
strength as spitting fire arched
around them. At last, Ferno righted
himself. Petra released her grip on
Tom's arm. She settled herself on
Ferno's scales and blew the hair from

her sweaty face.

"This is quite some ride!" she said.

"Tom!" Elenna cried, pointing towards a towering volcano ahead that was spewing a fountain of lava into the sky. They swooped towards it, molten rock cascading down all around them, smoking and sizzling where it struck the roiling lava below. Tom threw his shield above their heads, holding it over Petra and Elenna as best he could. Fist-sized drops of molten rock pummelled the wood as Ferno swept past the volcano. Others bounced harmlessly off his heatproof scales.

Suddenly, Ferno banked upwards. Tom's stomach lurched as they

climbed, leaving the plumes of gas and spitting lava far below. As Ferno levelled, Tom wiped the sweat from his face, drawing in a breath of cooler air. He let his shield fall, noticing the dragon's scale embedded in the wood glowing far brighter than usual – deep red, like a smouldering ember at the heart of a fire.

"Tom!" Elenna yelped. "Look at Petra!"

Tom turned to see the witch's eyes narrowed to bright red slits. She opened her mouth, and let out the grating squawk of a crow.

"Beware," Petra said.

Rourke's speaking through her!

Tom realised.

Petra lifted a finger and pointed upwards and ahead. "Berric and Quarg are close!"

DUEL IN THE SKY

Tom peered up through the buffeting
wind at the black and grey cloud
above, his sword clasped in his
hand. A flash of lighting slashed the
sky, blinding him for a moment. He
blinked to see Quarg's dark form
plunge from the clouds. The stone
dragon dived towards them, his huge
wings thrown back and his long neck

outstretched. Tom could just make out Berric's tiny shape crouched on the dragon's back.

Tom put his hand to the red jewel. *Be careful, Ferno. If Quarg turns you to stone, we will all perish.*

The fire dragon pumped his wings fiercely, climbing to meet Quarg's attack. Tom heard Petra squeal and Elenna suck in a breath. His own stomach flipped over and he almost lost his grip. He lowered his sword and clung for his life as the two dragons drew together, Ferno powering upwards and Quarg plunging like a deadly arrow. Soon, Tom could see the swirling blue fire in Quarg's eyes and the gleam of the dragon's curved teeth, getting closer by the moment. Just before the two dragons collided, Quarg's eyes flashed purple. Tom tensed his muscles, expecting to feel the blast of Quarg's magical energy – but instead, Ferno unleashed a stream of white hot flame. Tom saw Berric's eyes pop wide in terror. Quarg screamed with fury and tipped a wing, checking his fall and veering sharply away.

Ferno threw his wings open to their full span and levelled, letting the hot wind carry them onwards. Tom craned his neck to look back. He saw the purple dragon climbing, rising fast on an invisible thermal.

Quarg quickly reached the thick
bank of cloud above, then swooped
over in a loop and dive-bombed back
towards them, faster than ever. The
fire dragon surged over the swirling

lava, his massive wings pounding the scorching air. But Quarg had height on his side and was gaining fast as he plummeted.

His nostrils flared above his mouth of sharp, curved teeth. Berric craned forwards on Quarg's back, eyes flashing with triumph. Tom held tight to Ferno's back with his knees and lifted his sword, readying himself for the attack.

As Quarg reached them, his great talons snapped out, snatching for Elenna.

No, you don't! Tom lifted his shield and smashed the claw away, then stabbed for Quarg's leg. His sword struck the dragon's flesh with a stony *clang*, sending out sparks but leaving no mark.

Ferno dipped clear of Quarg's attack, banking dangerously close to the swirling lava and the random spurting geysers. Quarg followed, keeping pace just above them, swiping at Ferno's wings with his sharp claws as they flew. Time and time again, Ferno tried to climb away from the boiling, spitting lava and noxious gasses that engulfed them. But each time, Quarg headed them off, forcing them to stay low. Drops of sweat stung Tom's eyes. His damp clothes stuck to his skin, and heat and bitter fumes rising from the lava made his head swim.

On one side of him, Petra clung to Ferno's back, her face steaked with damp ash. On the other side, Elenna swayed and rubbed her eyes.

We have to get out of this heat, Tom realised.

He spotted a dark island of rock up ahead in the swirling sea of red and black. *Head for that dead volcano*, Tom told the dragon.

Ferno changed course in an instant, angling towards the cone of rock. Quarg let out a hiss of triumph, then beat his wings and shot upwards, vanishing into the clouds.

Ferno pressed on towards the island. Dark specks crowded Tom's vision, making his head spin.

We have to reach cooler air!

Finally, the island drew close. Ferno reached out his claws to touch down. At the same moment, Tom heard a screech, and glanced up. His stomach gave a sickening twist. Quarg was plummeting towards them, his deadly talons outstretched and Berric clinging to his scales like an insect.

Ferno let out an angry roar and veered upwards so suddenly Tom almost lost his grip. The fire dragon swerved away from the island, tipping his wings sharply to manage the tight turn. Petra slammed into Tom's side. Elenna screamed and

Tom looked to see her sliding off
Ferno's smooth scales, her hands
scrabbling for a grip. He reached
out and caught her wrist, grunting
with the effort as she hung below
him. He glanced back to see Quarg
level right behind them, his blazing
eyes fixed on Elenna.

No!

The stone dragon threw back his
wings, reached out a massive claw
and snatched hold of Elenna's legs.
Tom felt her body tugged away from
him, almost ripping his arm from
its socket, but he managed to keep
his grip. Elenna let out a cry of pain,
her face creased with agony. Tom
held on with all his strength and

pulled against the dragon. Elenna
struggled, trying to free her legs
from Quarg's talons. Tom's arm

burned with the strain, but he'd never let go.

He called on the magical strength of his golden breastplate.

"I've got you, Tom!" Petra cried, linking an arm through his to keep him steady.

Bubbling, swirling lava swept by beneath them – so close, Tom felt as if his clothes and hair might catch fire. Elenna's face was pale, and her eyes wide with terror.

"Tom!" she cried. "Let go!"

"Never!" Tom growled.

"You'll tear me in two!" Elenna shouted.

Tom looked at her body, tugged taut between Quarg's claw and his own hand, every muscle standing out on her arms and neck. He realised she was right. His heart clenched with anguish.

He opened his fingers and let go of Elenna.

Quarg let out a roar and swooped upwards. Horror and dread twisted in the pit of Tom's stomach as he saw

his friend carried away from him, higher and higher until she was a tiny doll in the stone dragon's claw.

FREEFALL

"No!" Tom roared. He struggled to his feet and called on the power of his golden boots to jump after his friend, but Petra yanked his arm, dragging him back.

"What are you doing?" she said. "If you jump now, you'll die – and so will Elenna!"

"But I can't just leave her to

Quarg!" Tom said hoarsely. Panic crushed his chest, making his breath come in painful gasps.

"Of course not!" Petra said. "And Elenna knows that. You'll figure this out – you always do. But plunging to your death won't help anyone."

Tom fought to control his rage and fear. Petra kept a firm grip of his arm, and held his gaze until his ragged breathing steadied.

Finally, Tom nodded. "You're right," he said. "Ferno – follow Quarg!"

The fire dragon banked upwards, surging towards the clouds. Tom felt his aching head clear as they hit cooler air. Petra narrowed her eyes, and Tom saw them change to a deep shade of red.

"That way!" she croaked, pointing east, towards a range of jagged mountains.

Ferno hit the dark cloud cover and hurtled onwards, climbing steadily through the thick, grey murk. Tom strained to see in the smoggy gloom. A jagged fork of lightning lashed past them, then another. Tom shielded his eyes against the blinding light.

"Keep going!" Petra croaked in Rourke's voice.

Then suddenly Ferno broke free of the cloud, bursting out into bright sunlight and clear blue sky. Quarg flew right ahead of them, sailing above the rolling clouds with Elenna dangling upside down from his claw. Tom saw her eyes widen as she spotted him.

Thank goodness she's alive!

Rourke flew above the stone dragon, fluttering around as if looking for an angle of attack. With his thoughts, Tom directed Ferno to swoop beneath the stone dragon.

"I'll get you down, Elenna!" Tom cried, looking up at his friend. Her face was as red as Rourke's feathers.

Tom drew back his sword and swiped at the scaled foot clasped about Elenna's legs. Sparks flew from the purple flesh, but Quarg

didn't flinch. Tom reached higher,
raking Quarg's softer underbelly
with the sharp tip of his sword.
Quarg let out a screech, flapped
his wings and climbed higher, out

of Tom's reach. Ferno opened his jaws, and sent a jet of white flame after the stone dragon. The fire hit the edge of Quarg's purple wing. Tom saw the skin there blacken and shrivel. Quarg let out a deafening roar of fury and pain. As the vast dragon swooped upwards and away, he opened his claw...

Panic clutched Tom's heart as Elenna plunged past him, too far away to reach. He didn't hesitate, but bent his knees and dived after his friend.

"Tom, no!" cried Petra.

Everything went dark for a moment as Tom dropped through ashy cloud. Then sweltering heat hit him like a fist as he plummeted out above the swirling sea of molten rock. Elenna was right below him, wheeling her arms and legs, trying to slow her fall.

"I'm coming!"Tom screamed, hoping his cracked voice would reach her though the wind. He glanced down at the deadly lava racing to meet them and almost called on the power of Arcta's feather to slow his fall. But he stilled the impulse and instead threw his arms back, streamlining his body, speeding up instead. Hot wind howled in his ears and whipped at his clothes. Shimmering waves of heat rose up to meet him,

making him narrow his eyes, but
Elenna was almost in reach. He
forced his arm out against the
blistering wind…

His fingers closed around her ankle.

Tom reached his free hand back and grabbed his shield, pulling it loose. As he held it above them, the wind almost tore the grip from his fingers, but he tightened his fist and gritted his teeth. At last he called on the power of Arcta's feather. With a terrific jolt that almost wrenched his outstretched arms from their sockets, the magic kicked in. The wind fell quiet around them, and they floated, slowly, towards the fiery sea.

Now Tom could see every detail of the churning lava clearly. He could see how cooling black rock and molten red flowed together, making

swirling patterns beneath their feet.
He could feel the deadly heat of
it rising towards them. He looked
frantically for somewhere to land
– any peak of solid rock. But there
was nothing. Tom swallowed hard.

What have I done?

Falling fast, or falling slow, the
lava would burn him and Elenna
just the same. Their Quest was over.

Jezrin had won.

1

7

MASTER AND APPRENTICE

Fear and helpless rage burned inside Tom as he and Elenna drifted ever closer to the lava below. The rising heat made his hands slippery with sweat, but even if Tom couldn't save Elenna, he wouldn't let her fall.

Caw! Caw! A flash of red crossed Tom's path.

Rourke!

A moment later, the sound of powerful wingbeats reached him over the hiss and bubble of the lava. He turned his head to see Petra riding towards him on Ferno. Relief

flooded through him in a dizzying wave. Ferno swooped beneath Tom and Elenna. Petra lifted both arms and caught Elenna round the waist. Tom let go of Elenna's ankle, and dropped onto Ferno's back behind the girls. He scrambled forwards as Petra helped Elenna turn and get into a sitting position. Ferno let out a triumphant breath of fire, then flew upwards, away from the scalding gases and spitting flames below.

"Everyone all right?" Petra asked as Tom took his seat beside her.

Elenna rubbed her face and blinked dust from her eyes. "Thanks to you two!" she said.

Petra smiled and shrugged. "Glad to be of service," she said. "Now, Rourke tells me Berric went that way." She pointed to a range of distant mountains, where the sea of lava finally seemed to give way to solid land. "I've got a score to settle with that little maggot – and so do both of you."

Tom nodded. "And maybe we'll have better luck facing Quarg on land than up here in the sky."

Ferno carried them until they reached the foothills of the mountains – a craggy plane of black volcanic rock, scattered with boulders and strange, twisted towers of cooled lava. The fire

dragon landed lightly, and extended
a wing to the stony ground. Tom,
Elenna and Petra climbed off and
looked about for any sign of Quarg.
Loose gravel crunched under
Tom's boots, and narrow streams
of smoke rose from fissures in the
rock around him. He drew his sword
and lifted his shield, noticing that
Ferno's scale embedded in the wood
burned brighter than ever.

Suddenly, Petra let out a
triumphant whoop.

"Look who I've found!" she said,
pointing over the craggy ground
towards the foot of the mountain.
Berric's slender figure lay sprawled
on the rock, his grey cloak tangled

about his body. "It looks like he fell off Quarg!" Petra said gleefully.

Tom started towards the twisted figure.

"Where are you doing?" Petra said. "He got what he deserved. Let him rot."

"I can't!" Tom said. "He might be on the side of Evil now, but if he's alive, I have to help him. You more than anyone should understand that people can change."

Petra scowled. "I've never been as bad as Berric!" she muttered.

Tom started towards Berric with Elenna at his side. The boy's white hair was dark with sweat and ash, but his face looked paler than ever.

Tom glanced around for any sign of Quarg. How badly burned was his wing? Was it possible the stone dragon had actually fallen into the lava himself?

Elenna dropped to her knees at Berric's side, and put a hand to his wrist.

"He's alive!" she said.

A winged shadow flitted across Berric's body. Tom's breath caught in his throat and he looked up, expecting to see Quarg. But instead, he spotted Rourke's red plumage outlined against the cloud. Petra made a strange wheezing sound. Tom turned to see her eyes glowing red as she stared up at the sky.

"The Beast is close!" she squawked, in Rourke's rasping voice.

Suddenly, Tom heard a smack and a yelp of pain from behind him. He turned to see Elenna sprawled on the ground and Berric gone.

"Elenna!" Tom stepped towards his friend, who was grimacing and clutching her head.

BOOF! Berric leapt from behind a low rock, barging shoulder-first into Tom's legs, knocking him from his feet. Tom landed on his belly with a gasp of pain. His sword and shield flew from his grip. He scrambled to reach them, but Berric got there first. Tom gritted his teeth in fury, pushed the pain from his mind and leapt to his feet. Berric circled him, smiling.

"Not so brave now without your weapons, are you?" Berric said.

Tom ran his eyes over the boy's scrawny form, taking in the awkward way he gripped the sword and shield. "Maybe not," Tom said, "but I'm more than a match for you." Tom leapt forwards, swinging his foot in a high arc and kicking the sword out from Berric's hand. He grabbed a fistful of the boy's tunic and yanked him forwards and off balance. Then he wrenched his shield from Berric's hand, and thrust him away.

Jezrin's apprentice stumbled backwards over the uneven ground, tumbling over and smacking his head. Tom stepped forwards and stood over the boy. As Berric's eyes blinked into focus, Ferno let out an angry growl.

"We have company!" Petra shouted.

Tom looked up to see Quarg diving towards them, a cloaked figure on his back. Tom left Berric where he lay, and ran for his sword. He snatched it up and lifted it high, ready to face the Beast. Elenna raced to his side, shaking her head, as if to clear dizziness. She notched an arrow to her bow.

Petra joined them. She chanted an incantation, drawing two balls of powerful white energy into her hands. Ferno gave a great roar of fury and turned to face the stone dragon as it came in to land.

Quarg extended his curved talons and touched down on the rocky ground. The cloaked figure dismounted and threw back his hood, revealing keen black eyes, sharp angular features and a thin-lipped evil smile. *Jezrin.*

Berric stumbled past Tom towards the wizard. "Master!" he cried. "I brought them to you, just as you asked!"

Jezrin's face twisted in a snarl. He lifted his hand. "Quarg!" he snapped. "Silence that fool!"

Two beams of sizzling purple energy shot from Quarg's eyes and slammed into Berric's chest. A bright lilac glow surrounded Berric for

an instant. When it faded, Tom saw
Berric's body had turned to cold,
hard stone.

"That's for failing me!" Jezrin
hissed at the statue of his apprentice.
Then his eyes flickered from Elenna,
to Petra, to Tom. "Now, who's next?"

Elenna let her arrow fly. It hit Quarg's scaled chest, and fell harmlessly to the ground. The dragon turned his swirling eyes on Elenna, but Ferno growled and flapped into his path.

A blast of white energy shot

towards Jezrin from Petra's hands, but Jezrin gave a careless wave, and the light vanished before him, as if it had struck an invisible shield.

Jezrin took a long, shining dart from his cloak and drew back his arm, smiling at Tom.

Tom lifted his shield, ready to catch the dart. But at the last moment, the Evil Wizard changed his aim. He flicked his wrist, sending the dart slicing towards Ferno.

"Watch out!" Tom cried, too late.

The sharp, silvery missile struck Ferno right between the eyes and sank deep into the Good Beast's scaled flesh. He swayed, then slumped to the ground with a crash, his eyelids closed.

"No!" Elenna cried, her voice filled with anguish. Tom felt an echoing cry deep inside him.

"He won't be bothering us any more," sneered Jezrin.

THE DEADLY WOUND

Hot rage flooded through Tom. He reached out for Ferno with the red jewel, but sensed nothing.

Is he dead?

Tom lunged towards Jezrin, his sword raised ready to strike.

Jezrin didn't flinch. "I wouldn't do that," he said, pointing at Tom.

Quarg reared up with a venomous hiss, and fixed his blazing eyes on Tom. Elenna's arrow whistled past and clattered against Quarg's damaged wing, but the dragon didn't even seem to notice.

Purple energy sizzled toward Tom. He leapt aside just as – *crack!* – the ground exploded into dust and chips of stone.

"Leave him alone!" Petra cried, two balls of white fire blazing in her palms. But Jezrin was faster.

ZAP! A blue bolt of crackling energy surrounded Petra, making her judder and shake.

Jezrin cackled. "Your magical power is nothing compared to mine,

young witch!"

Twang! An arrow sliced through
the folds of Jezrin's cloak, making
him stagger back and pinning
the trailing fabric to the ground.

Jezrin's magical beam faltered.
Petra sank to her knees, but Jezrin
sent another beam sizzling towards
her.

"No!" Tom shouted. He lowered
his head and charged towards
Jezrin, slamming shoulder first into
the wizard's body and knocking him

to the ground.

Jezrin's head cracked sickeningly against a rock, and his eyes rolled up in his head. Released from Jezrin's magic, Petra collapsed on to her side and lay still. Tom lifted his sword above the fallen wizard, ready to strike.

"Look out!" Elenna cried.

Tom turned to see Quarg's long neck extend towards him, the dragon's eyes swirling with purple fire. Without thinking, Tom threw up his shield.

The purple beam hit the wood, and Tom froze, expecting to feel the cold stiffness of stone encasing his body. But instead, the bright energy rebounded off his shield, straight back at Quarg. It hit Quarg's damaged wing and let out a flare of dazzling violet light. With a strange, crackling sound, like ice dropped in water, the blackened wing turned grey and hard.

Petra was wrong! Ferno's scale does work against Quarg's fire!

Quarg lifted his long neck and fired another blast of purple energy at Tom. Tom's reflexes took over, and he angled his shield to catch the ray. The blazing beam struck

the shield exactly where Tom had
hoped, reflecting straight back into
Quarg's eyes. Loud cracks and pops
filled the air. Quarg's neck started
to flex, but froze in mid-movement.
Hard grey rock encased the dragon's
head, spreading down his scaled
neck and over his body. In less than
a heartbeat, the Beast was still – a
cold statue of lifeless stone.

Jezrin howled with fury and
scrambled to his feet, a ragged hole
torn in the hem of his cloak, and
blood trickling down his face. "My
servants may have all let me down,"
Jezrin screeched, spit flying from his
thin lips, "but you will not escape
me next time, boy! I will drink from

the Well of Power, and destroy all you hold dear."

The wizard took a vial from inside his cloak and dashed it against the ground. A sickly green light flared around him. When it faded, Jezrin was gone.

Tom let out a sigh, and took in the devastation. A monumental statue with outstretched wings stood where Quarg had been. A second, far smaller statue, huddled closer to the ground. Petra was lying silent, struck down by Jezrin's magic, and a brave Good Beast had fallen, his wings folded limply across his back. Even with the stone dragon defeated, Tom could feel nothing but empty sorrow. Elenna crossed to his side and put a hand on his shoulder.

"None of this is your fault," she said. "This is Jezrin's doing."

A hoarse croak came from above them, and Rourke appeared, flapping towards his mistress. To Tom's surprise and joy, Petra stirred. She pushed herself up on one arm, then rubbed her eyes. Rourke flapped up onto her shoulder.

"Clever Petra!" Rourke croaked. Petra stroked Rourke's head. As she started to rise, her gaze fell on Quarg's statue. Her eyes shot wide open with alarm. But then she frowned and stepped towards the dragon, running a hand over its hard grey scales.

"You turned him to stone?" Petra asked.

Tom nodded.

"Look!" Elenna said, pointing at Quarg's head.

Tom looked up, to see a jagged fissure appear between Quarg's eyes. A crackling, creaking sound seemed to be coming from the stone. Petra leapt back.

Horror stirred in Tom's gut as he saw the fissure spread, covering the statue with thin black lines. A loud splitting sound echoed around them, and one sharp horn fell from above the dragon's eye to the ground.

Petra lifted her hands, drawing
two balls of magic into her palms.
Elenna raised her bow.

"Don't!" Tom said, stepping before
them. With his hand to the red jewel
in his belt, he felt no anger from
Quarg.

"He means us no harm," Tom said.
"In fact, I think he's grateful."

Quarg flexed his neck and wings
and the rest of the stone that
encased his body fell away, tumbling
to the ground. As soon as Quarg was
free, he turned his eyes on Ferno's
still body. Tom felt a wave of sorrow
come from the stone dragon. Quarg
lowered his giant head and nuzzled
Ferno's jaw with his snout, making

a soft, grunting sound. Then he looked at the silver dart embedded in Ferno's skull. Quarg opened his jaws slightly, and breathed a gentle stream of purple fire on to the dart.

The silver metal shimmered and melted, tricking away across the black ground.

Ferno's orange eyes flickered open. Tom, Elenna and Petra watched in awed silence as Quarg stepped back, and Ferno lifted his head. The fire dragon got slowly to his feet, flexed his neck and wings, then let out a puff of orange flame. The two dragons extended their long necks towards each other, then bowed their heads and stepped apart.

Quarg flapped his wings hard, once, twice, and powered away into the sky, leaving behind a mound of rubble and a single purple horn. Tom picked the horn from the pile.

"Keep that safe," Petra said. "It's Quarg's gift to you."

"What now?" asked Elenna.

"Let's head back to sunny Avantia," said Petra. "I never liked dragons very much anyway."

Tom tucked the purple horn into his belt and shook his head. "Jezrin is searching for the well. We have to stop him, whatever it takes."

"Well said," Elenna replied. "But what about Berric? We can't just leave him here to die, but I don't fancy taking him with us, either."

Petra looked at the cowering statue of Jezrin's apprentice and rubbed her hands together. "I could turn him into a swamp leech for you," she said, "or a puddle of slime mould, or...no, wait! A warty stink toad!"

Tom frowned at Petra and shook his head, one finger raised. "Second chances, remember?" he said.

Petra bunched her fists. "But surely you're not just going to let him walk free?" she said.

"No," Tom said, "that would be far too risky." He crossed to the statue, and inspected the smooth stone that covered Berric's open mouth. Tom lifted his sword, and chipped a hole in the stone. A gasp of breath came from inside.

"Release me!" Berric's reedy voice piped through the hole.

"Sorry," Tom said. "You're going to have to figure that out for yourself." Then he turned and walked away, followed by a string of Berric's curses.

Petra and Elenna hurried to Tom's

side as he strode towards Ferno. "I think that little challenge should keep Berric busy for a while," Tom said. He sheathed his sword then turned from the ocean of bubbling fire inland towards the craggy mountains. "The Quest is on," he said.

THE END

1

CONGRATULATIONS, YOU HAVE COMPLETED THIS QUEST!

At the end of each chapter you were awarded a special gold coin.
The QUEST in this book was worth an amazing 8 coins.

Look at the Beast Quest totem picture inside the back cover of this book to see how far you've come in your journey to become

MASTER OF THE BEASTS.

The more books you read, the more coins you will collect!

Do you want your own
Beast Quest Totem?
1. Cut out and collect the coin below
2. Go to the Beast Quest website
3. Download and print out your totem
4. Add your coin to the totem
www.beastquest.co.uk/totem

Don't miss the next exciting Beast Quest book, KORVAX THE SEA DRAGON!

Read on for a sneak peek...

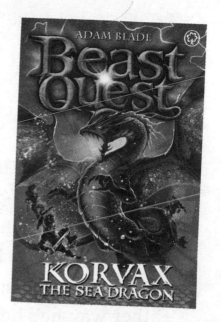

SNOWLANDS OF THE NORTH

Tom stood on a barren hilltop, gazing across the kingdom of Drakonia. All around him, volcanoes spewed smoke into the sky, and rivers of lava trailed down rocky mountains. Using the power of the golden helmet, Tom scanned far into the distance.

"There's no sign of Jezrin," he said, sighing.

Petra placed her hands on her hips. The witch's red crow, Rourke, squawked on her shoulder. "Either he's using magic to hide from you, or he cast a speed spell," Petra said. "Either way, he's heading for the Well of Power."

"Maybe Berric knows which way he went," said Elenna.

Tom turned to the stone figure of Jezrin's apprentice, hands frozen over his face. Under the Evil Wizard's control, the dragon Quarg had encased Berric in a layer of rock.

"He would never tell," said Tom,

shaking his head. "And we can't waste time trying to free him." He sat down on a boulder, worry churning in his stomach. "The moment Jezrin drinks from the well, he'll become invincible," he said.

"Well, obviously, I could always track him," said Petra, feeding a bit of stale bread to Rourke.

Elenna raised her eyebrows. "Why didn't you say that before?"

Petra shrugged. "You didn't ask."

"How can you?" said Tom, urgently.

"Every wizard leaves a trail on the air when using magic," said Petra. She wrinkled her nose. "Jezrin's scent is most powerful. I could smell him two kingdoms away! Sulphur, boiled cabbage and bad feet."

Elenna grimaced. "Rather you than me," she muttered.

"Then your nose can guide us," Tom said to Petra. He led them down the hilltop to where Ferno lay waiting. The great fire dragon's wings were folded along his ridged back, his scales reflecting the red glow of the volcanoes. Drakonia was the kingdom where all dragons came from, and only dragons knew how to cross into the realm. Jezrin and Berric had used Quarg, and Tom had summoned the Good Beast Ferno to carry them there.

Tom climbed on to the Beast's back and spoke to him through the red jewel of Torgor. *We need your help again, old friend.*

Petra and Elenna settled themselves between Ferno's spiny ridges. The witch sat up, sniffing.

"Jezrin went that way," she said, pointing north.

"North, Ferno!" Tom commanded. The huge Beast rose to his feet and spread his wings. Tom felt a rush of air on his face as the dragon leaped high, wings beating steadily as he carried them above the hills.

On they flew, passing beyond the land of volcanoes until they soared over mountains whose foothills were dusted with snow. The air became cold, and although the fire dragon's body was warm beneath them, Tom could see his breath gusting white as they sped along. He turned to Petra.

Rourke still clung to her shoulder, the wind ruffling his red feathers.

"One thing puzzles me," Tom said. "How did Jezrin first gain control of Quarg?"

"It's said that Jezrin's master stole a dragon's egg from Drakonia," Petra replied. "Jezrin raised Quarg from a hatchling."

"That would make it far easier for him to control the poor Beast," said Elenna thoughtfully.

Petra raised her chin and sniffed. "Jezrin's close," she said.

Tom guided Ferno lower, soaring through a low valley. Tom scanned the ground rushing past beneath him. He spied a line of marks in the snow. "Footprints!" he cried. "They're man-sized. But they're too far apart."

"Jezrin is using a leaping spell," said Petra, squinting at the prints.

Elenna grinned. "He's still not as fast as a dragon, though."

Just then, Tom felt Ferno shudder beneath him as the fire dragon's wings faltered.

"I think you spoke too soon," said Petra.

Tom felt a rush of worry for his old friend. *Something's wrong.*

"Is it the cold?" asked Elenna, as Ferno struggled along, dipping lower at every wingbeat.

"He might be tired," Tom said. "It's been a long flight with no rest."

It is more than tiredness, said Ferno, in Tom's head. *My wings feel leaden and my heart labours. Some dark magic is working against me.*

Set us down now, said Tom. *We can't let you get hurt.*

Tom clung on grimly as the ground raced up to meet them. Ferno's great back arched, and his wings spread back. But the dragon wobbled in the air, and they hit the ground hard, the dragon's forelegs collapsing beneath him. Snow and ice gushed into Tom's face, blinding him. He could hear Elenna and Petra yelling in alarm as Ferno bumped along the valley floor.

At last, he slithered to a stop in a deep trough of snow.

Tom wiped his eyes as Ferno rose to his feet. His great body shuddered as he lifted his head and shook the snow off his scales.

"Quite a ride!" Petra gasped. "I thought we were done for!"

Read

KORVAX THE SEA DRAGON

to find out what happens next!

Fight the Beasts,
Fear the Magic

Do you want to know more
about BEAST QUEST?
Then join our Quest Club!

Visit
www.beastquest.co.uk/club
and sign up today!

Are you a collector of the Beast Quest Cards?
Visit the website for further information.